Dear Parents:

P9-DIW-520

Congratulations! Your child is taking the first steps on an exciting journey. The destination? Independent reading!

STEP INTO READING® will help your child get there. The program offers five steps to reading success. Each step includes fun stories and colorful art or photographs. In addition to original fiction and books with favorite characters, there are Step into Reading Non-Fiction Readers, Phonics Readers and Boxed Sets, Sticker Readers, and Comic Readers—a complete literacy program with something to interest every child.

Learning to Read, Step by Step!

Ready to Read   Preschool–Kindergarten
• big type and easy words • rhyme and rhythm • picture clues
For children who know the alphabet and are eager to begin reading.

Reading with Help   Preschool–Grade 1
• basic vocabulary • short sentences • simple stories
For children who recognize familiar words and sound out new words with help.

Reading on Your Own   Grades 1–3
• engaging characters • easy-to-follow plots • popular topics
For children who are ready to read on their own.

Reading Paragraphs   Grades 2–3
• challenging vocabulary • short paragraphs • exciting stories
For newly independent readers who read simple sentences with confidence.

Ready for Chapters   Grades 2–4
• chapters • longer paragraphs • full-color art
For children who want to take the plunge into chapter books but still like colorful pictures.

STEP INTO READING® is designed to give every child a successful reading experience. The grade levels are only guides; children will progress through the steps at their own speed, developing confidence in their reading. The F&P Text Level on the back cover serves as another tool to help you choose the right book for your child.

Remember, a lifetime love of reading starts with a single step!

Copyright © 2020 by Tad Hills
Text by Elle Stephens
Art by Grace Mills

All rights reserved. Published in the United States by Random House Children's Books, a division of Penguin Random House LLC, New York.

Step into Reading, Random House, and the Random House colophon are registered trademarks of Penguin Random House LLC.

Visit us on the Web!
StepIntoReading.com
rhcbooks.com

Educators and librarians, for a variety of teaching tools, visit us at RHTeachersLibrarians.com

Library of Congress Cataloging-in-Publication Data is available upon request.

ISBN 978-0-593-17789-1 (trade) — ISBN 978-0-593-17790-7 (lib. bdg.) —
ISBN 978-0-593-17792-1 (hardcover) — ISBN 978-0-593-17791-4 (ebook)

Printed in the United States of America
10 9 8 7 6 5 4 3 2 1

This book has been officially leveled by using the F&P Text Level Gradient™ Leveling System.

Random House Children's Books supports the First Amendment and celebrates the right to read.

Penguin Random House LLC supports copyright. Copyright fuels creativity, encourages diverse voices, promotes free speech, and creates a vibrant culture. Thank you for buying an authorized edition of this book and for complying with copyright laws by not reproducing, scanning, or distributing any part in any form without permission. You are supporting writers and allowing Penguin Random House to publish books for every reader.

STEP INTO READING®

1 STEP READY TO READ

Rocket Loves Hide-and-Seek!

Pictures based on the art by Tad Hills

Random House 🏠 New York

Rocket plays
hide-and-seek.

He looks for Owl
and Bella.

He looks

in a tree.

He looks

under the bushes.

He looks one way.

He looks the other way.

He looks up.

Rocket finds Owl!

"It is my turn to hide,"
says Rocket.

Rocket hides
in the flowers.

Bella finds him
right away.

Rocket hides
behind a tree.

Owl finds him
right away.

Rocket hides
in many places.

His friends
find him
every time.

Rocket is sad.

"I am not
a very good hider,"
he says.

"It is just that you
are bigger than us,"
Bella says.

"I have an idea!"

Owl says.

Owl gets leaves.

Bella makes mud.

They cover Rocket
in mud and leaves.

He is ready to hide!

Rocket hides
in the bushes.

Bella does not
find him.

Rocket hides

in a hole.

Owl does not
find him.

The friends play
together all day.

Rocket loves
hide-and-seek!